Dinner with OLIVIA™

adapted by Emily Sollinger   illustrated by Guy Wolek

SIMON AND SCHUSTER

Based on the TV series OLIVIA™

First published in Great Britain in 2010 by Simon and Schuster UK Ltd
1st Floor, 222 Gray's Inn Road, London, WC1X 8HB
A CBS Company

Published in the United States by Little Simon, an imprint of Simon & Schuster Children's Publishing Division

ISBN: 978 1 84738 610 6

Printed in Great Britain

10 9 8 7 6 5 4 3 2 1

www.simonandschuster.co.uk

After a busy morning at school, it was finally time for lunch. Olivia joined her friends Julian and Francine in the cafeteria.
"A cream cheese, pickle and raisin sandwich!" Olivia announced, as she opened her lunchbox. She took a big bite and smiled.

Julian had a peanut butter calzone for lunch. "Want a taste?" he asked.
"I don't think so," said Olivia.
"No, thank you," said Francine, as she took her lunch out of her backpack.
It was in a shiny purple box.

"What kind of lunchbox is *that*?" asked Olivia.

"It's called a bento box," said Francine. "My parents got it for me in Japan!" Each compartment held a different kind of food: chicken satay, baby corn, star fruit . . . and that wasn't all. "Look at this!" Francine said proudly, as she took her utensil out of the box.

"Wow," Olivia and Julian said at the same time.

"Cool spoon!" said Julian.

"Cool fork!" said Olivia.

"It's both – it's a spork!" said Francine. Olivia and Julian were amazed.

Francine dug the spork into her bento box and pulled out a Brussels sprout.
"And this is a Brussels sprout. It's from Belgium . . . in Europe!"
"You *like* Brussels sprouts?" asked Julian.
"They're delicious!" Francine answered. "At my house, everything is perfectly
delicious!"

Then Francine had an idea. "Olivia, you simply *must* come to my house for dinner!"
"Really? Will there be Brussels sprouts?" Olivia asked.
"Of course not!" said Francine. "We never eat the same food twice in one year."
Olivia was happy to hear that. "I'd love to come. Thank you."
"Perfect!" said Francine. "I'll ask my mother to call your mother."

At home that night, Olivia decided she needed to practise her manners before going to Francine's house for dinner, so she hosted her own dinner party. She reminded her guests to always say "please" and "thank you" and to put their napkins on their laps. She told them never to fall asleep at the table. She made sure they remembered to chew with their mouths closed.

"At a fancy dinner party, everything needs to be perfect!" Olivia told her guests.

Olivia imagines what dinner at Francine's house would be like. She pictures a fancy party at a mansion in the English countryside, with waiters on roller skates serving pink lemonade in tall glasses with curly straws and monkeys juggling fruit . . .

"Olivia! Dinnertime!" called her mother,
interrupting her daydream.

At the dinner table,
Olivia's brother Ian
slurped his spaghetti,
splattering her dress
with tomato sauce.

One of his meatballs fell to the floor where Perry, the dog, picked it up in his mouth.

"Perry, that's *my* meatball," Ian yelled, chasing him around the table.

Perry gobbled it up . . . with his mouth open . . . leaving tomato sauce everywhere.

"I am quite sure they don't eat like this at Francine's house," Olivia groaned.

The next day, Olivia walked
to Francine's house with her
mother and brothers.
"Have fun tonight, Olivia,"
her mother said, "and don't
forget to invite Francine to
our house for dinner too."

"OUR HOUSE?" said Olivia, horrified. She looked over at her brothers. Ian was blowing bubbles in his juice box and William's face was smeared with jam.
She imagined what dinner at her house would look like to Francine. . .

"Welcome to our humble . . . cave!"

At Francine's house, Olivia gave Francine's mother a bouquet of flowers.

"Why, thank you, Olivia, but I have a rule about no fresh flowers in the house," said Francine's mother. "They make such a mess when their petals drop!"

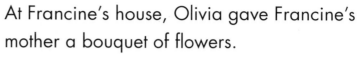

"Be sure to wipe your feet, Olivia. We mustn't get footprints on the white carpet!"

Like any good guest, Olivia told funny stories. Just as Francine's father was telling her it wasn't polite to tell jokes at the dinner table, Olivia saw Francine's mother come out of the kitchen with bowls full of . . .

Brussels sprouts!
Olivia looked at the pile of green in her bowl. To be polite, she decided to take a very small bite. Maybe Francine was right. Maybe Brussels sprouts *were* delicious. Maybe not.
Olivia quickly reached for her water glass to wash it down but . . . Oops! She knocked one of the Brussels sprouts out of her bowl and it rolled off the table and onto the white carpet.

Francine's mother and father were not pleased. Olivia and Francine were told to sit at the kids' table.

"Are you cross with me?" asked Francine.

"Why would I be cross?" asked Olivia.

"Because of the Brussels sprouts and the no jokes at the table," replied Francine. "And, well, I was afraid you wouldn't be my friend anymore!"

"Of *course* we're still friends!" replied Olivia. "And you should come to dinner at my house."

Later that week, it was finally Francine's turn to come to Olivia's house for dinner. It was spaghetti night. Again.

"I've never seen anyone do that before," said Francine,
as she watched Ian slurp his spaghetti.
"Try it!" said Ian.
"I'll race you!" said Olivia.
Turns out, Francine was a natural!

That night, as Olivia's mother tucked her into bed, Olivia had one thing on her mind. "Can we have spaghetti again tomorrow night?" she asked.

"That's a little too soon, don't you think?" said Olivia's mother.

"Okay. Goodnight, Mum." Olivia yawned.

"Sweet dreams, Olivia," whispered her mother, as she turned off the light and closed the door.